Copper and Charcoal go to School by InnovoNZ Limited

Published by InnovoNZ Limited, PO Box 47240, Ponsonby, Auckland 1144, New Zealand.

For information about special discounts available for bulk purchases, sales promotions, fund-raising and educational needs, contact InnovoNZ Limited via the contact form on www.Millvy.com or message via facebook Millvy.com.

Currently available on Amazon as an ebook and in paperback copy. Follow author Eleanor Kit / Michelle K Wade to get updates on other Millvy™ books and products coming soon.

First edition

ISBN: 978-0-9951493-4-2 [Kindle]

ISBN: 978-0-9951493-5-9 [Paperback]

ISBN: 978-0-9951493-6-6 [Epub]

ISBN: 978-0-9951493-7-3 [Hardcover]

Cover design by Bryony van der Merwe

Book formatting by Bryony van der Merwe

Illustrations by Lizette Duvenage

Photographs by MK Wade, IL Jury and iStock

Editing by Sandra Paton

Author Eleanor Kit (pen name for Michelle K Wade)

Book 1 in Copper Charcoal (Millvy's Brothers) series.

Book 1

Copper & Charcoal go to School

Millvy's brothers arrive

ELEANOR KIT

Millvy, a silver Maine Coon cat, arrived home to find a strange looking white box tied with a red ribbon sitting on the floor.

A black nose was poking out of a hole at the front of the box and a golden tail was wagging through a hole in the back.

Through the other holes could be seen a mixture of black and golden fur.

What could it be?

"Woof, woof, woof!" said the box.

Millvy's Mum came in and pulled the ribbon to open the box.

Out popped two puppies. One was golden in color and one was a blackish color.

"Millvy, these are your new brothers," explained Mum. "Meet Copper and Charcoal."

Millvy watched them from a safe distance.

LATER THAT DAY…

"Hello Millvy," Copper said shyly. "Why haven't you got a tail?"

"Well," Millvy replied, "one day I woke up and it just wasn't there. It had gone missing, and I have been looking for it ever since."

"Maybe we could help you find it when we grow bigger," offered Charcoal.

"Yes, I would like that," Millvy purred.

Copper and Charcoal quickly adjusted to their new family and the household routines.

"Copper! Charcoal!" called Mum. "Today we are going to start your basic manners training so you can get ready to go to school. Come along!" she said.

Into the car they went with their family. They soon arrived at the Dog Training Centre.

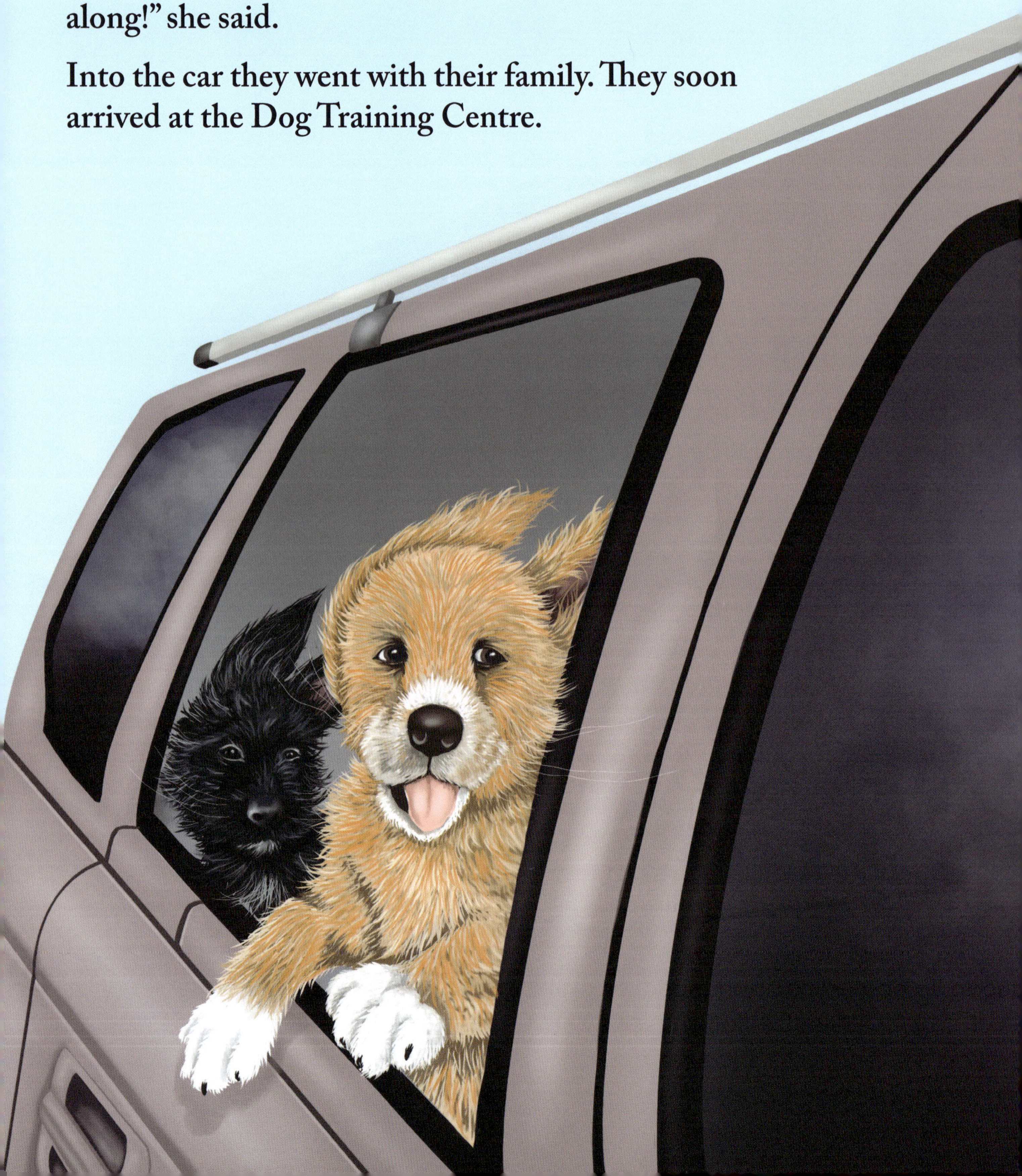

When Copper and Charcoal joined the training class there were about eight other dogs of different types and sizes. These dogs were all a similar age to them and new to training too.

The teacher had treats and soon all the dogs felt very welcome.

Over the next eight weeks, Copper and Charcoal learned many new dog commands as part of the basic manners training, starting with:

Sit

Stay

Watch me

Come

In-between lessons, they enjoyed practicing at home with their family.

Copper and Charcoal learned both the word and the hand signals for all the new commands.

Learning these would help keep them safe when outside the house.

They would help them be well-behaved so Mum could take them to places like school, and on walks and family adventures.

The basic manner commands they needed to learn included:

Lie down

Stop

Drop it

Leave it

Rollover

Heel

Certificate of Completion

Bark Academy

This is to certify

Copper

has successfully completed
BASIC MANNER TRAINING PROGRAMME

and has been awarded the following mark 98%

Signed

Date May 2021

After two months of basic manners training, Mum announced, “Today is a special day. You have passed your training and now you can start school. Your school is called Bark Academy.”

Certificate of Completion

This is to certify

Charcoal

has successfully completed

BASIC MANNER TRAINING PROGRAMME

and has been awarded the following mark *92%*

Signed ______ Date *May 2021*

Mum drove them to their new school on their first day.

Bark Academy's Head Teacher, Kristie, greeted them and introduced Mum to their day teachers, Lukus and Colleen.

The teachers took Copper and Charcoal to their new classroom. It was very exciting. There were lots of new dogs to meet.

Copper and Charcoal joined in the games and liked playing with the new toys.

Teachers Lukus and Colleen kept a close eye on them to make sure everyone played together nicely. The teachers gave out treats when Copper and Charcoal showed they could use their manners: Come, Sit, Stay.

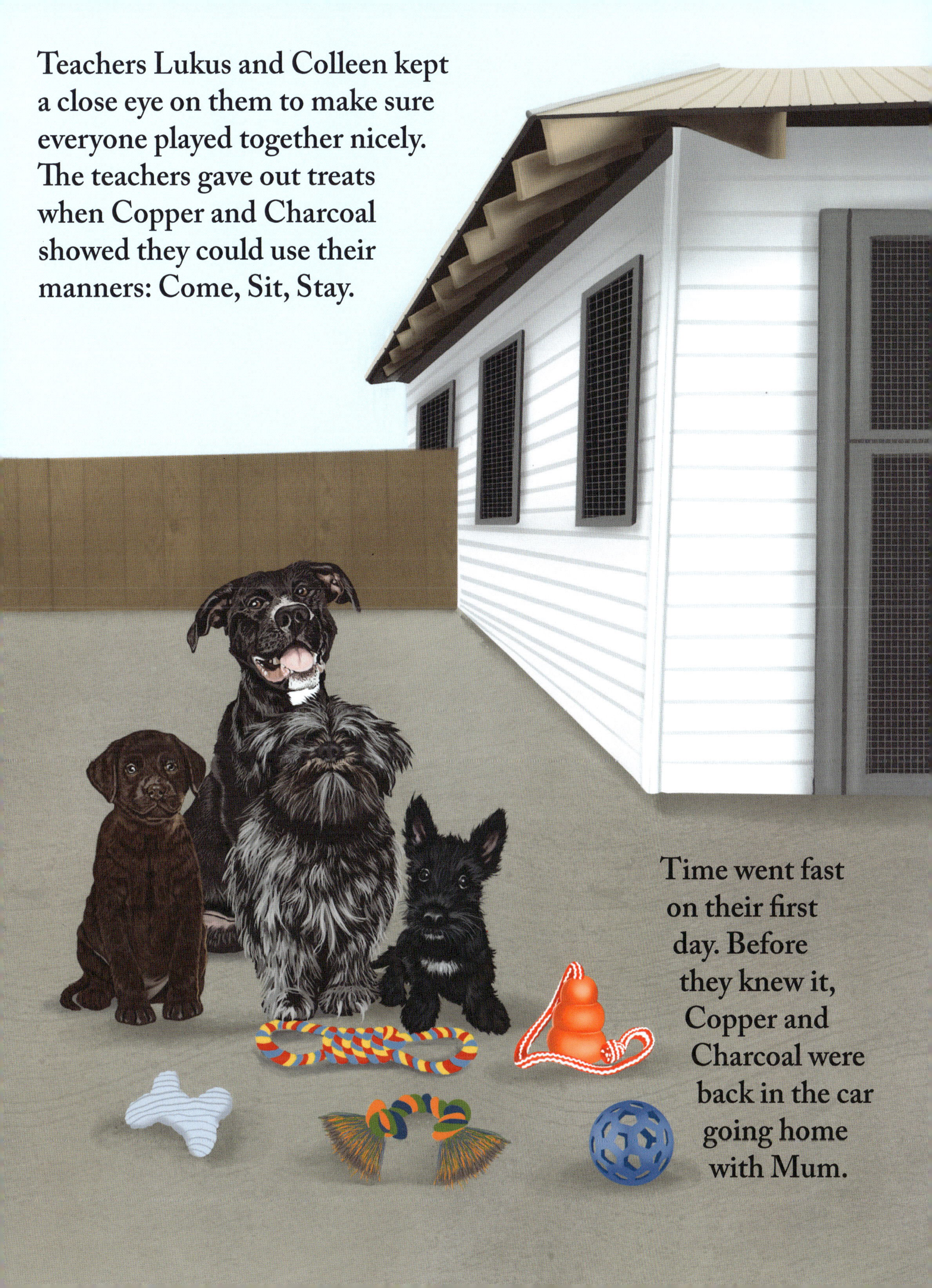

Time went fast on their first day. Before they knew it, Copper and Charcoal were back in the car going home with Mum.

That night Millvy asked his brothers how they got on at school.

"It was so much fun," Copper told him. "I made lots of new friends and their names are Guinness, Lola, Baxter, Beau, Miko, and Chica." Copper sounded happy.

"And how did you get on, Charcoal?" asked Millvy.

"Well," replied Charcoal. "I didn't make a particular friend and some of them called me Barky Charky. My teacher, Colleen, asked them to stop."

"Oh dear," said Millvy. "Were you being loud?"

"I was very excited, so I suppose I was barking a lot more than normal," admitted Charcoal.

"What do you think you could do differently tomorrow?" asked Millvy.

"Perhaps I could try being quieter, listen more and use my inside voice, then they might have time to get to know me better."

"Yes, that's a great idea," agreed Millvy.

Charcoal felt much happier now that he had a plan.

When they came home from school the next day, Charcoal had a big smile on his face.

"Guess what, Millvy? I made a special friend and her name is Lulu." Charcoal announced excitedly. "It was her first week at school too and she likes my bark! The teacher even took a picture of us for the parents' Facebook page."

"That's marvellous!" said Millvy, "How did you get on with the other dogs in your class?"

"Well, I minded my manners like we talked about, and I had three dogs ask me to play tug rope games with them. So, it was a great day!"

A FEW MONTHS LATER …

"This week is photo week at school," said Mum. "After the photos are taken, you will both get a report card from the teachers. I think we really need to get you to the groomers to get haircuts and toenails clipped before your photos are taken."

Off they went in the car and soon they arrived at the groomers.

"Welcome Copper and Charcoal," Hazel the Groomer said warmly. "Follow me!"

They went into a room which had baths and tables and other bits of equipment. There was even a hairdryer like Mums!

They had never been to a groomer before, so they felt nervous. Hazel was very nice and she put them at ease. She gave them a treat when they sat and did as she asked.

Soon they are being washed, clipped and blow dried.

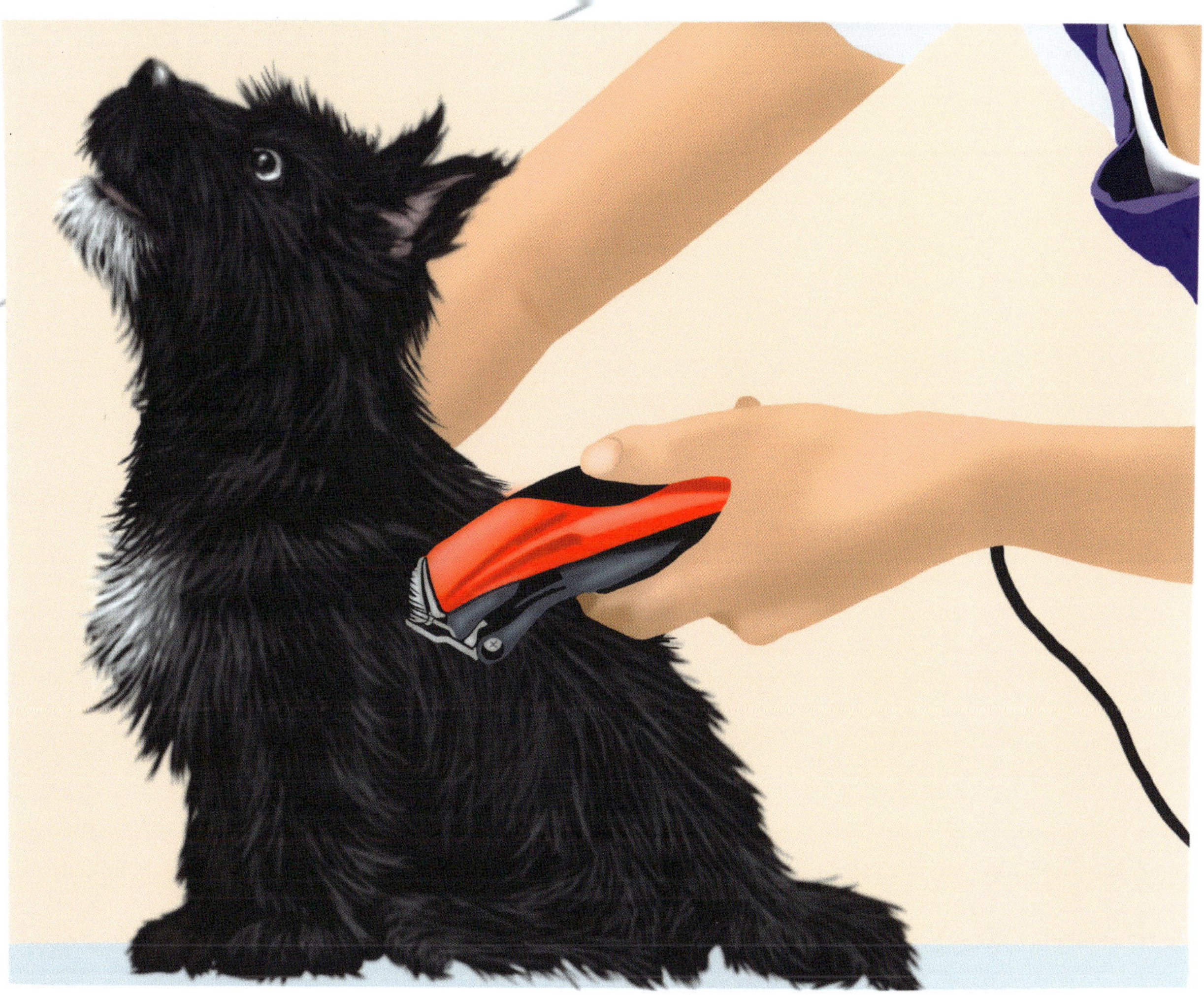

"Wow!" exclaimed Mum when she came to pick them up. "You look fabulous and smell beautiful! I hope you stay that way for your photo in a few days' time."

TWO DAYS LATER...

Copper and Charcoal were called out of class for their turn with the photographer. Because they were brothers, they got to have a picture together as well as one on their own.

"Say *Rabbits!*" called the photographer to try to get them to smile.

"You both sat very still and listened to the photographer," Teacher Lukus praised them on the way back to class. "Here is a treat for your good behaviour."

The next day as they made their way out of school, Mum collected a packet from the front counter.

When they got home, Mum pulled out Copper and Charcoal's photos and report cards.

Mum had a big smile on her face as she read out the teachers' comments:

> Copper is forming lots of new friendships and making the most of every day with huge energy for ball games and class activities. We are reminding him to work on his loud barking when he gets too excited.
>
> Charcoal is really improving his recall and getting quicker to come when called. We love his big grin and he continues to make new friends.

Millvy looked at the photos.

"Hey, you guys look quite handsome in these pictures," he said. "And well done on your school reports!"

That night Mum said, “I am so proud of your first year at school, and how well you behaved with your classmates and your teachers. Tonight, we will celebrate with your favourite dinner food."

Copper enjoyed roast chicken while Charcoal loved his possum patties.

After their delicious dinners, Copper and Charcoal had big smiles on their faces. They settled down to sleep, exhausted from all the excitement of the day, and started dreaming about next year at Bark Academy ...

Meanwhile, where is Millvy going?

The end.

Copper & Charcoal

reality notes

Millvy and his brothers

MILLVY

Copper and Charcoal have a big brother, a silver Maine Coon cat, called "Millvy".

Millvy no longer has a tail – read all about this in 'Millvy's Reality Notes' in Millvy's Missing Tail – Book 1.

Who is the elder of Millvy's two brothers - Copper or Charcoal?

HERE IS A PICTURE OF NEW ZEALAND

Can you find it on the world map?

Can you find Auckland city?

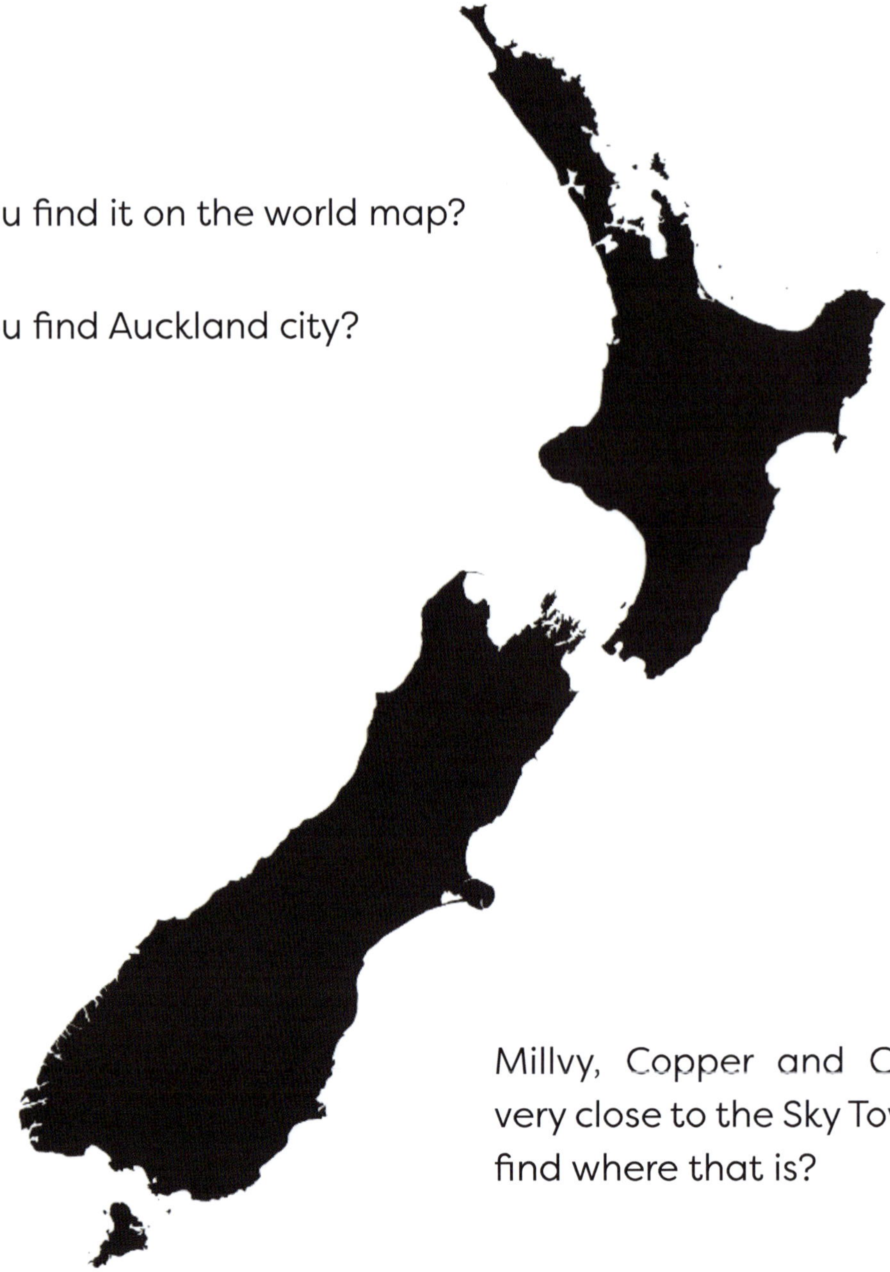

Millvy, Copper and Charcoal live very close to the Sky Tower. Can you find where that is?

CHARCOAL

AGE Charcoal was born on 19 December 2014.

Charcoal was the first puppy to join the family. His family chose him from a pet store in Auckland, New Zealand. Charcoal was 8 weeks old when he came and quite excitable – especially when he saw Millvy. He was too busy for cuddles in his first year and a bit stubborn about training but likes to sleep by his human at night.

Charcoal in his back yard in the first week with his family.

Charcoal in his first year at school.

NAME

The name 'Charcoal' was chosen due to his color. He is a lighter shade of black with speckles of white here and there. His name is in keeping with the family theme of naming their pets after colours of chemical elements, minerals, or natural materials. [1]

DOG BREED

Charcoal is a cross breed – this means his parents are different types of dogs or breeds.

Charcoal's Mum is a 'West Highland White Terrier' commonly known as a 'Westie'

Charcoal's Dad is a black 'Scottish Terrier' commonly called a Scottie.

These two types of dogs - Westies and Scotties – are considered a 'small' dog breed.

Both the **Scottie** and **Westie** breeds were originally bred by farmers to help them manage vermin problems. They are great for getting into burrows and sniffing out prey, such as badgers, foxes, rabbits, and other vermin such as rats.

[1] Millvy's passport name is Silver but his family have nick named him Millvy.

Charcoal loves going into the bush or forest to sniff out new animals and finds mice in his own back yard.

Charcoal has definite traits from the Westie and Scottie breeds. He is very devoted to his humans and will cock his head to the side when they talk to him. He will chase anything that moves – including Millvy! He can also be very stubborn and often doesn't want to come when called. These are his Westie traits.

Scottish terriers are often described as a big dog in a little dog's body. They are feisty, independent, and sometimes excitable. Charcoal's nature is certainly like this and at school he is in a class with all the big dogs. He needs to be reminded to use his inside voice as he gets too excited. These are his Scottie traits.

While we do not know Charcoal's parent's they would look something like the pictures on this page.

This picture is what Charcoal's parents might look like if they were out playing together.

COPPER

AGE Copper was born on 09 January 2015.

Copper's family chose him from a breeder in Auckland, New Zealand. He was 8 weeks old when he came to live with his family. Copper loved his cuddles and food! He was so happy to have a new dog brother already in the home to play with, but he had to learn to share his toys.

Copper in his crate when he first arrived at his family

Copper in his first year at school. He grew big quite fast.

NAME

The name Copper was chosen due to his reddish gold fur colour that reminded the family of the mineral copper.

DOG BREED

Copper is also a cross breed – this means his parents are also different types of dogs or breeds.

Copper's Mum is a red 'Border Collie' called Cassie. She would have looked something like the picture.

Border Collies were originally used for working with livestock, most commonly herding sheep, and cattle. These days they still do this job but because they are intelligent and highly trainable, they are also used as service dogs in many industries such as police work, border customs detection for drugs, and for search and rescue missions.

Copper doesn't have any animals to herd but he is very protective of Charcoal and is always looking out for him.

Border Collies also do very well in various canine sports, including obedience and agility.

Copper's Dad is a 'Golden Retriever' called Rocky. He would have looked something like the picture.

The **Golden Retriever** was originally bred to help hunters with finding birds or other game and bringing them back undamaged.

Retrievers are active and fun-loving animals with a very patient demeanour which makes them good family dogs and therapy service dogs. They are one of the most popular dog breeds in the world as they are so friendly, charming, and tolerant. They like to have a job to do.

Copper thinks his job is to look after his family and he will call out with little woofs if his humans are out of sight in another part of the house.

These two types of dogs - Border Collie and Retriever - are considered to be a 'large' dog breed. These breeds like a lot of exercise.

These pictures are what Coppers parents might look like if they were out playing.

Millvy's Missing Tail Series

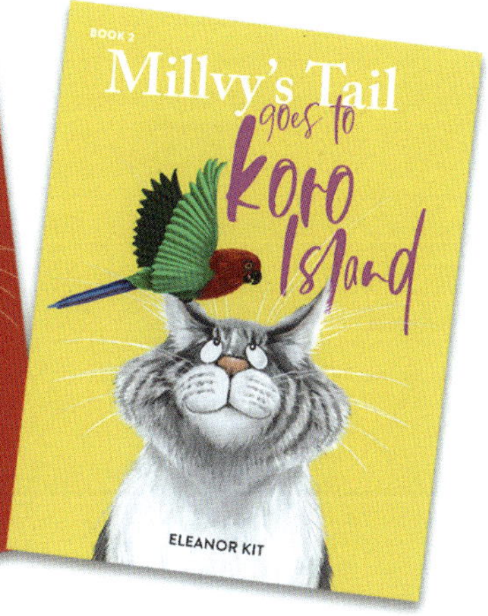

Millvy Education Series

Copper and Charcoal Series (Millvy's brothers)

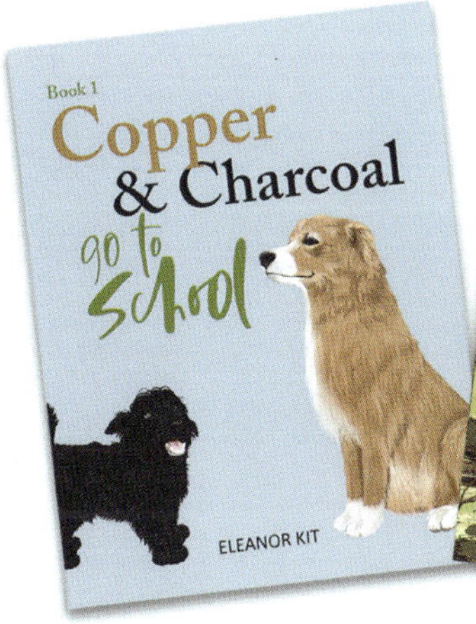

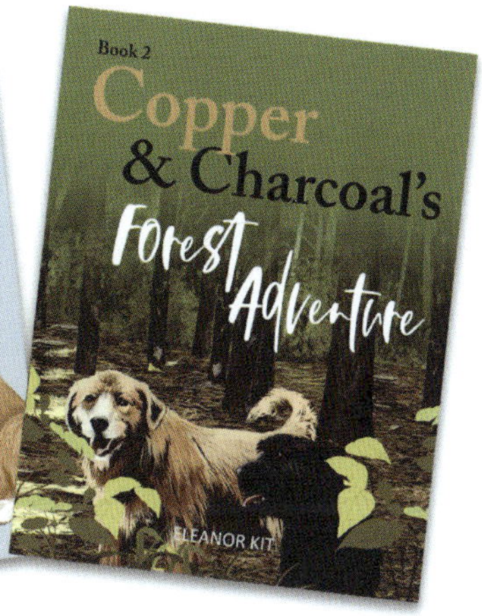

Go to www.Millvy.com

to find out where you can buy more books in the Millvy range.

Printed in Great Britain
by Amazon

33474164R00023